W9-CAP-609

A COLD NIGHT

A CHRISTMAS FABLE

By Emanuele Bertossi

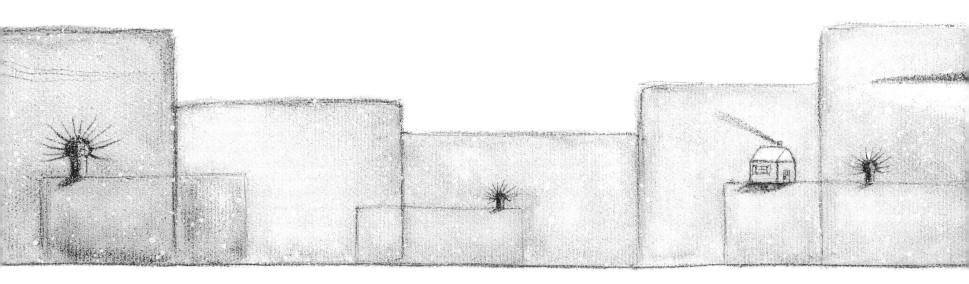

SPARK
HOUSE
FAMILY
sparkhouse.org

Minneapolis

"Look!" Cow said. "It's snowing!"

"I'm not surprised," Donkey said. "The sky has been gray and cloudy for the last two days."

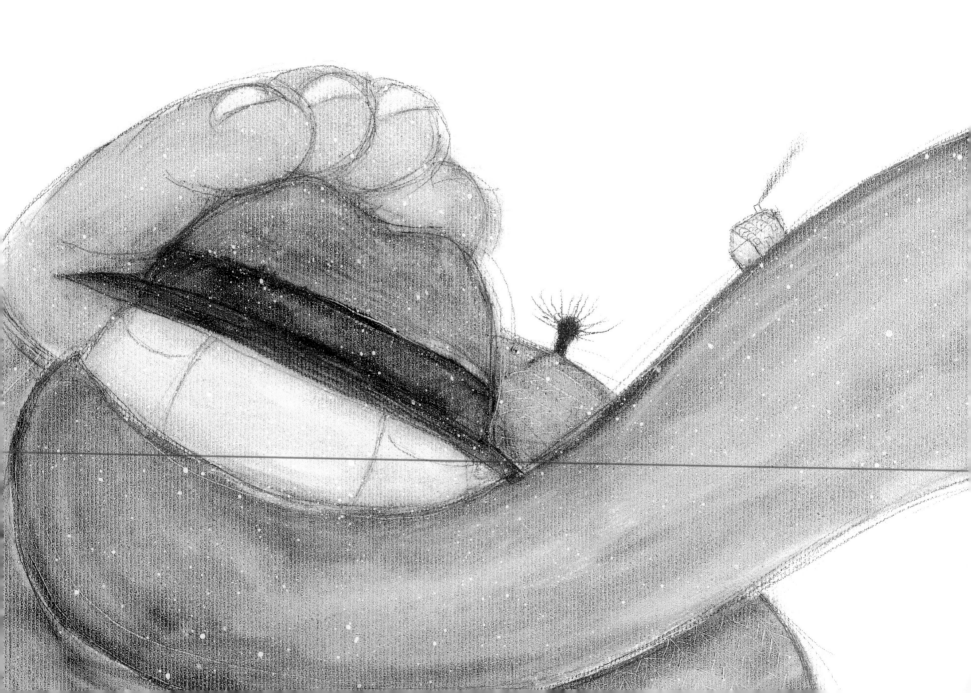

"We're lucky," Cow said. "We have a warm stable, a trough full of food, and dry hay to sleep in."

"You're right," said Donkey. "I feel sorry for anyone who doesn't have shelter tonight."

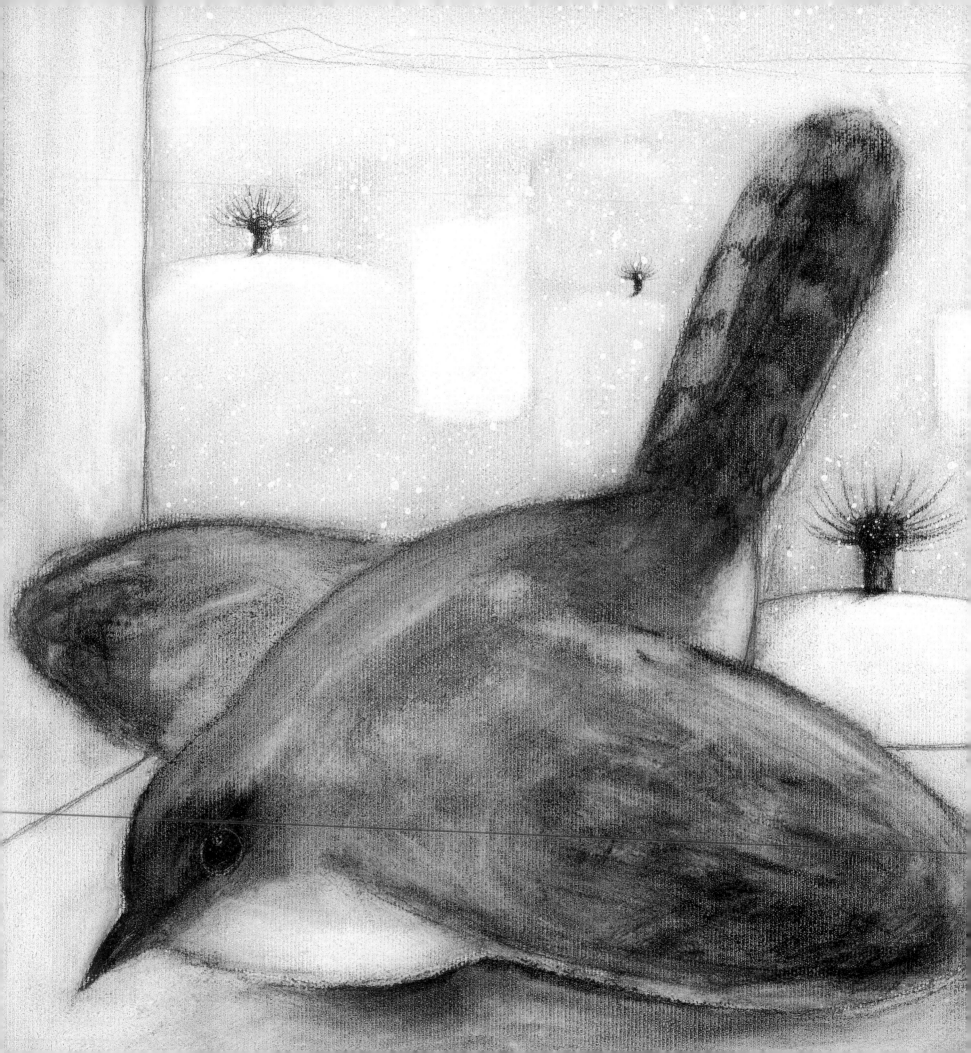

While they were talking, Wren flapped down and shook the snowflakes off her wings.

"May I stay here tonight?" she asked, shivering. "It's so cold outside!"

"Of course," said Cow. "Come inside and get warm."

Outside, the snow kept falling. Here and there, animals looked up at the sky and scurried for shelter.

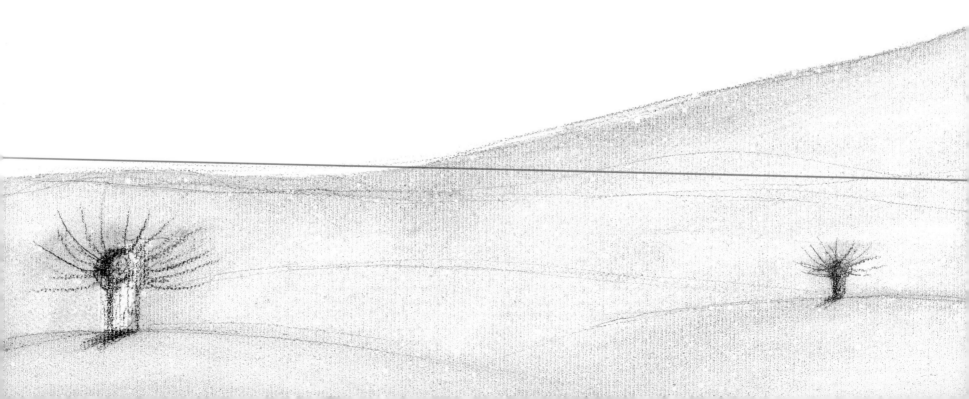

Soon there came a *tap, tap, tap* at the door.

"That must be Woodpecker," said Donkey. "We should let him in."

Woodpecker hopped inside the stable and huddled up with the other animals to keep warm.

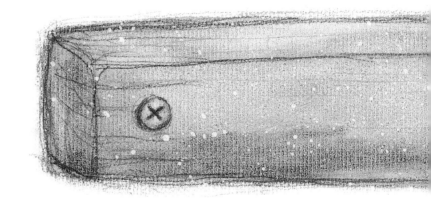

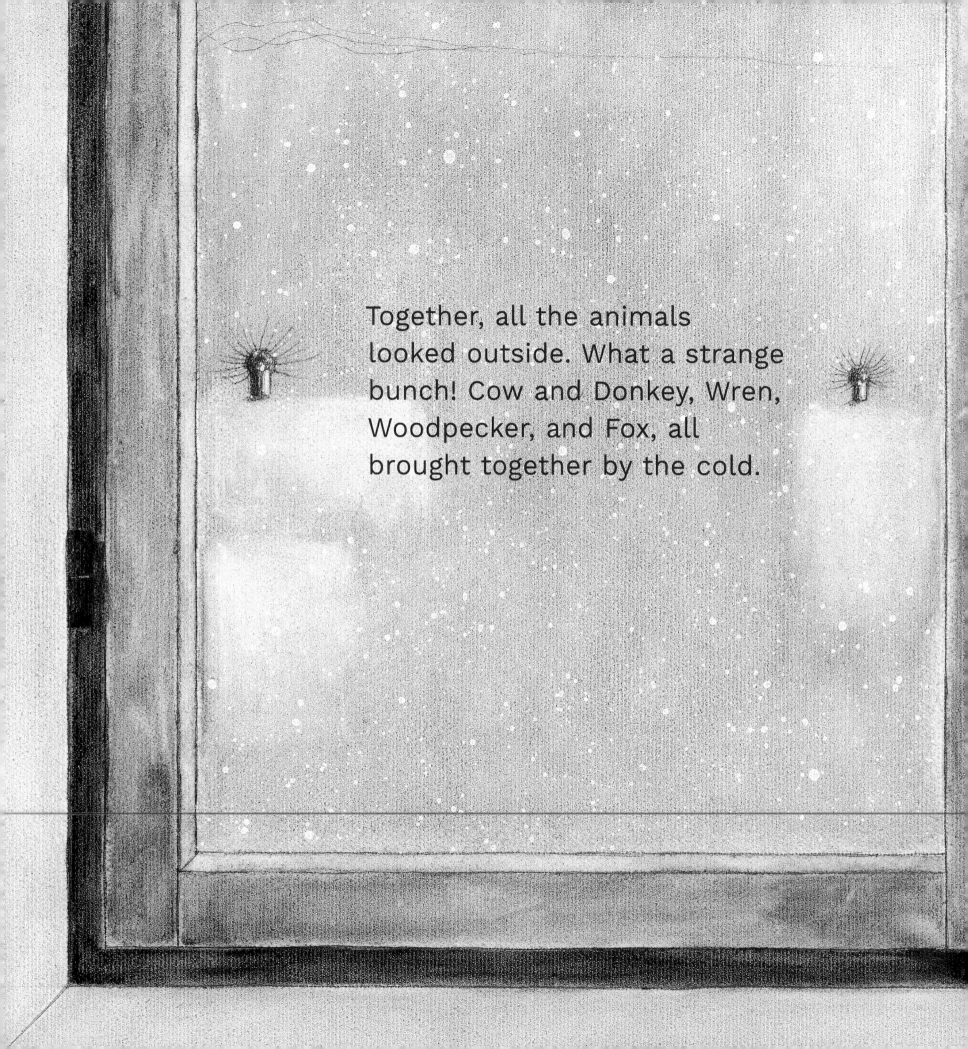

Together, all the animals looked outside. What a strange bunch! Cow and Donkey, Wren, Woodpecker, and Fox, all brought together by the cold.

Suddenly, Wren spotted something. "Look!" he chirped. "There, on the path. It's a man and a woman."

"What a terrible night to be traveling!" Fox cried. "Why are they out in this cold?"

"Maybe they had no choice," Cow said.

"What will happen to them?" asked Donkey. "I hope someone gives them a place to stay."

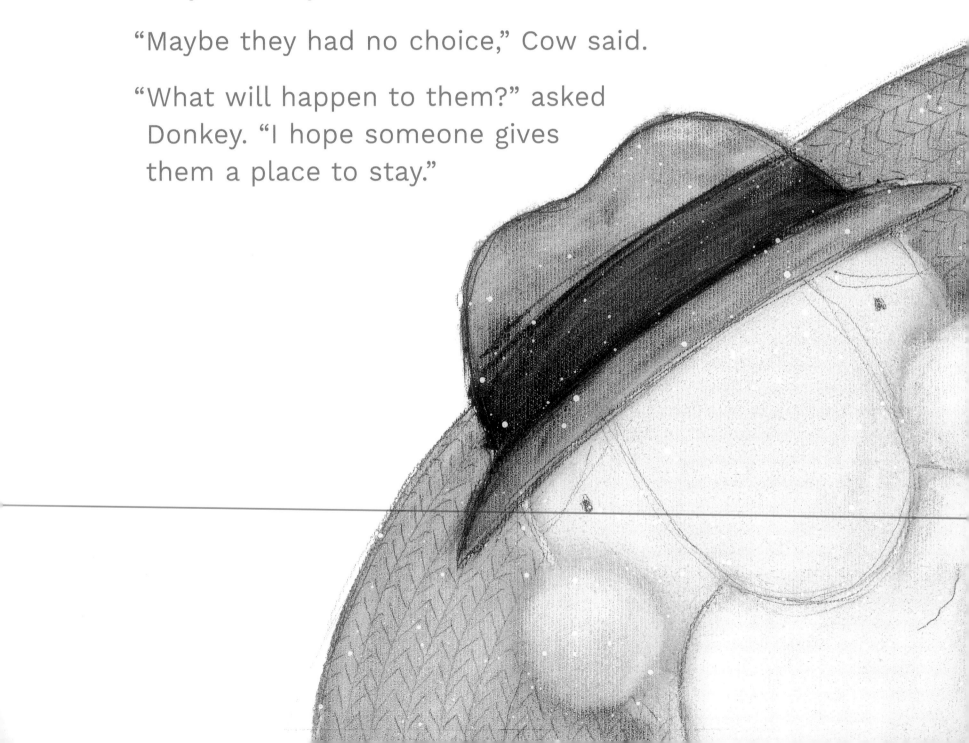

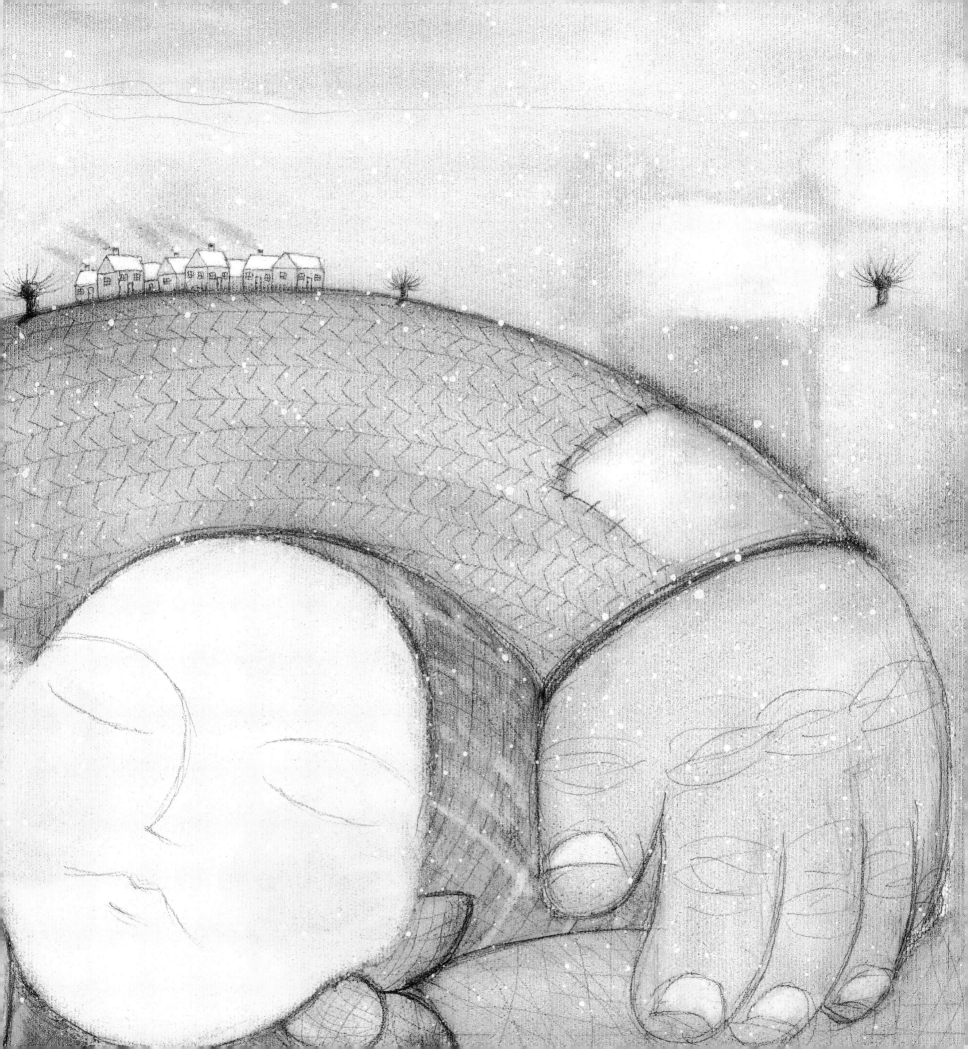

Outside, the night grew colder. The wind howled. Warm inside the stable, Cow, Donkey, Wren, Woodpecker, and Fox were all quiet, their thoughts whirling like snowflakes on the wind.

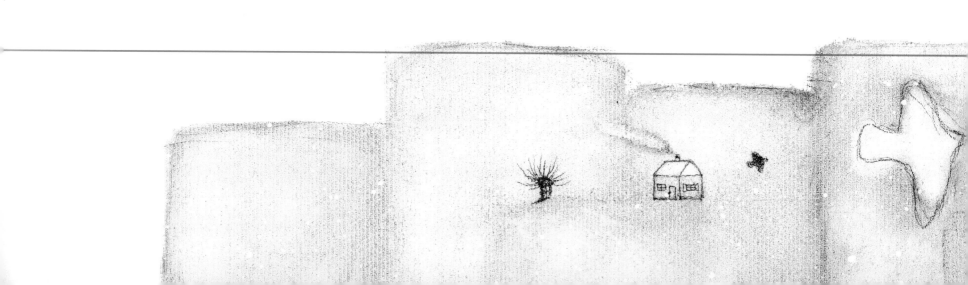

Soon, it was dark, and they heard a knock on the door.

"Who could that be?" asked Donkey.

The door creaked open. The man and the woman stood in the doorway.

"Can we come in?" the man asked timidly. "We're cold, and my wife is pregnant. We knocked on every door in the village, but nobody would let us in."

Without saying a word, the animals parted to let the man and the woman inside.

Later that night, the woman gave birth to a baby boy. Cow, Donkey, Wren, Woodpecker, and Fox listened to his cries, then watched over him as he fell asleep on the hay.

Outside, a star appeared above the stable.

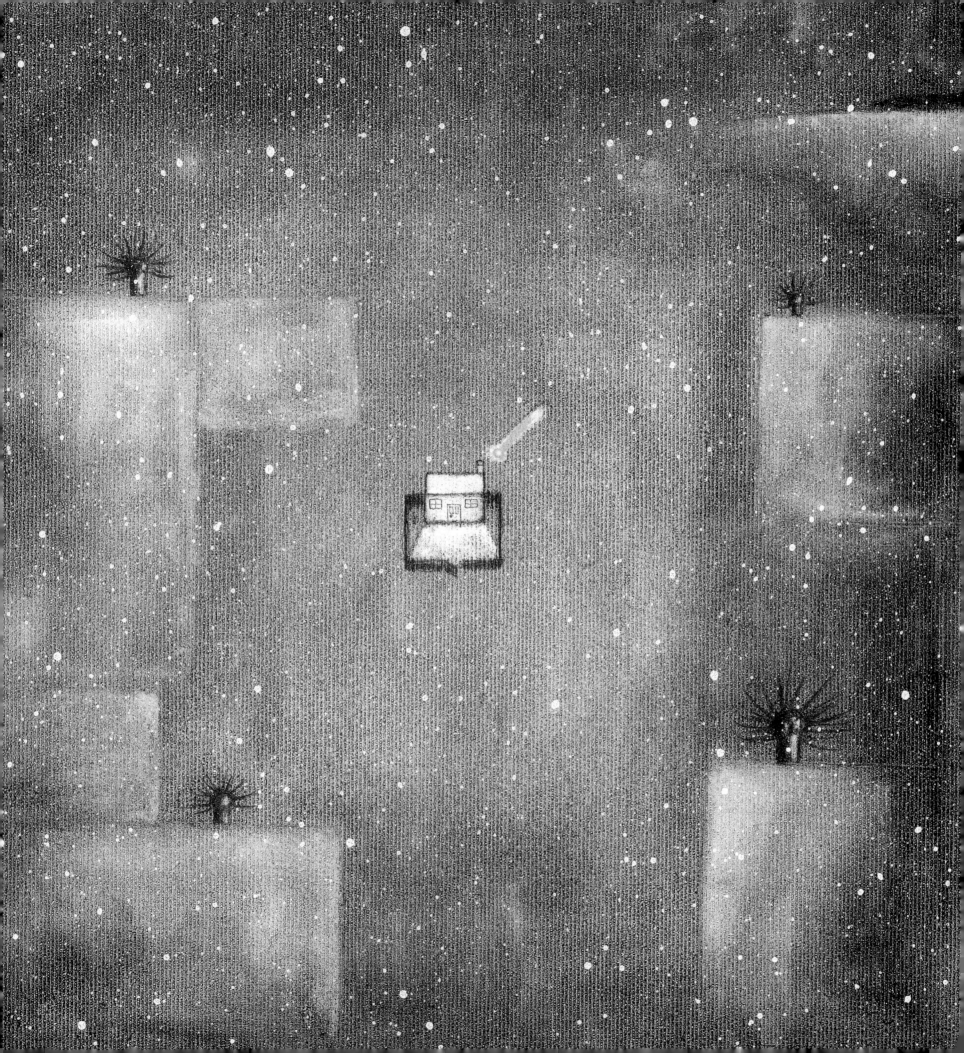

Original title: *Neveade* by Emanuele Bertossi
First published in Friulian, Italy

ISBN: 978-1-5064-2496-5
Library of Congress Control Number: 2017947355

VN0004589; 9781506424965; JUL2017

Sparkhouse Family
510 Marquette Avenue
Minneapolis, MN 55402
sparkhouse.org